DON'T SLAM THE DOOR!

DORI CHACONAS

illustrated by

WILL HILLENBRAND

CANDLEWICK PRESS

Please don't slam the door!
  Don't slam that old screen door!
A slamming door will wake the cat,
  and heaven knows, we don't want that,
so please don't slam that door!

Please don't wake the cat!
      Don't wake that naughty cat.
He'll play in Mama's knitting chair.
      He'll roll those yarn balls everywhere.
Now look! You woke the cat!

Cat, don't knot the yarn!
    Don't knot Ma's knitting yarn!
You've rolled it all around the house.
    Go find a ball! Go chase a mouse!
You're messing up Ma's yarn!

Ma, don't knit with knots!
   This yarn is full of knots.
Knitted socks should not be lumpy.
   Lumpy socks will make Pa grumpy.
Please don't knit with knots!

Pa, don't wear those socks!
  Don't wear those lumpy socks.
Those knots will never go away.
  You'll limp and hop and yelp all day!
So don't put on those socks!

Pa, don't hop and yell!
    Don't hop and yip and yell!
Look out! You bumped the honey hive!
    The bees are swarming, sakes alive!
Just stop that awful yell!

Bees, don't swarm and sting!
    Don't swarm and swoop and sting.
Now see! You've stung that old brown bear.
    You've frightened him, but you don't care!
It's not polite to sting!

Don't run through the barn!
  Hey, Bear! Not through the barn!
You'll give those cows an awful scare,
  you silly, bee-stung, scaredy-bear.
Oh, yikes! He's in the barn!

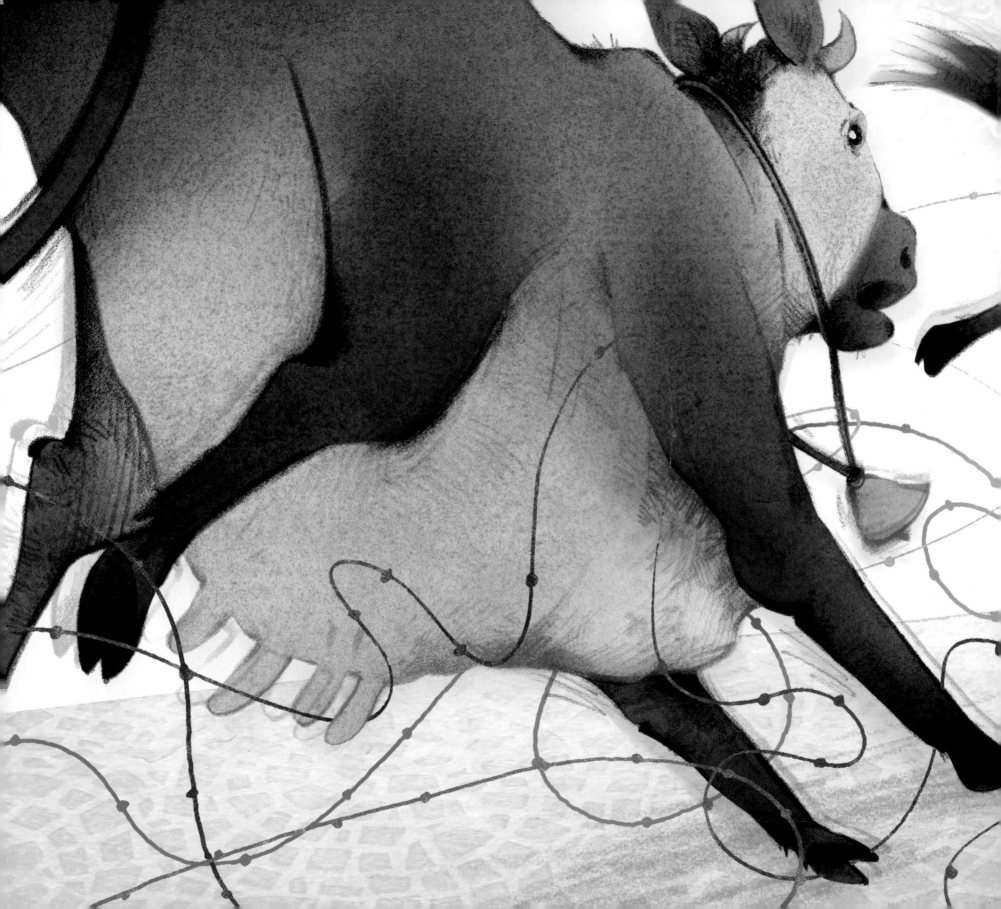

Help! Here come those cows!
They won't stay in the barn.
They're running to the house instead.
They're hiding in the feather bed,
all tangled up in yarn!

Those clunky-lunky cows must go!
They've covered Pa with feather snow.
The bees are buzzing round the floor.
The bear is snuffling at the door!
Ma's yarn is in an awful heap.
That cat will never go to sleep!

I'M GOING TO COUNT TO FIVE!
I want you bees back in the hive!
I want you, Bear, to go away!
I want you cows back in the hay!
Now SCOOT! SCAT! and on your way....

Don't *ever* slam that door!
A slamming door will wake the cat,
    and heaven knows, we don't want that!
We've been through this before!

I CAN'T TAKE ANY MORE!

For the whole Kozak clan
D. C.

To Annamarie, thanks for the knitted socks!
W. H.

Text copyright © 2010 by Dori Chaconas
Illustrations copyright © 2010 by Will Hillenbrand

First edition 2010

Library of Congress Cataloging-in-Publication Data

Chaconas, Dori, date.
Don't slam the door! / Dori Chaconas ; illustrated by Will Hillenbrand. —1st ed.
p. cm.
Summary: A cumulative, rhyming tale of a slamming door which wakes a cat,
setting into motion an absurd chain of events and resulting in chaos.
ISBN 978-0-7636-3709-5
[1. Stories in rhyme. 2. Doors—Fiction. 3. Animals—Fiction. 4. Humorous stories.]
I. Hillenbrand, Will, ill. II. Title. III. Title: Do not slam the door!
PZ8.3.C345Don 2010
[E]—dc22   2009015254

10 11 12 13 14 15 LEO 10 9 8 7 6 5 4 3 2 1

Printed in Heshan, Guangdong, China

This book was typeset in Aunt Mildred.
The illustrations were done in mixed media.

Candlewick Press
99 Dover Street
Somerville, Massachusetts 02144

visit us at www.candlewick.com